KB196127

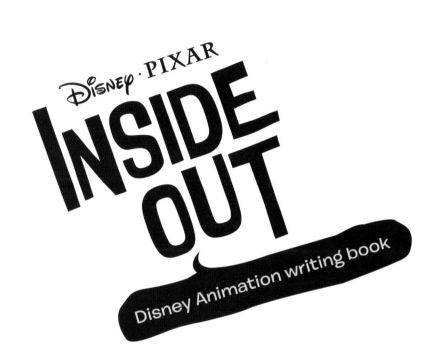

Disney · PIXAR

INSIDE OUT

Disney Animation writing book

글 안드레아 포스너 산체스 | **그림** 앨런 뱃슨

더모던
Themodern

MEET *the* CHARACTERS

RILEY

The girl who moved to San Francisco. She misses her life in Minnesota: the happy times she spent playing ice hockey on the frozen lakes, the friendships she made, and the happy memories of her family.

Riley is just entering puberty, and her sudden move leaves her adrift in an unfamiliar environment.

Riley's sudden move causes her to wander, but it also causes her to grow.

JOY

Always a **CHEERFUL OPTIMIST**, Joy will do whatever it takes to make sure that her girl, Riley, has an awesome life. Working with fellow Emotions Anger, Disgust, Fear, and Sadness, Joy has her tried-and-true plans to keep Riley happy and protect her Sense of Self.

ANGER

Though he can be pretty hot-headed and **EXPLOSIVE**, Anger is willing to risk anything and take any chances, all to get the very best for Riley.

DISGUST

Protect Riley's physical and emotional health by saying no to disgusting things.

FEAR

Fear may be **OVERPROTECTIVE** of Riley, but that's only because he's always terrified. Fear's job is to keep Riley as **SAFE** as he can, so he's always on the lookout for danger.

SADNESS

Besides being pretty sad, Sadness is not very confident in herself, but Joy knows that Sadness **HAS WHAT IT TAKES** to help make Riley's life amazing.

This is Joy. She is an Emotion who lives in Riley's mind. Ever since Riley was born, Joy has been in charge of keeping her girl happy. Joy is very good at her job!

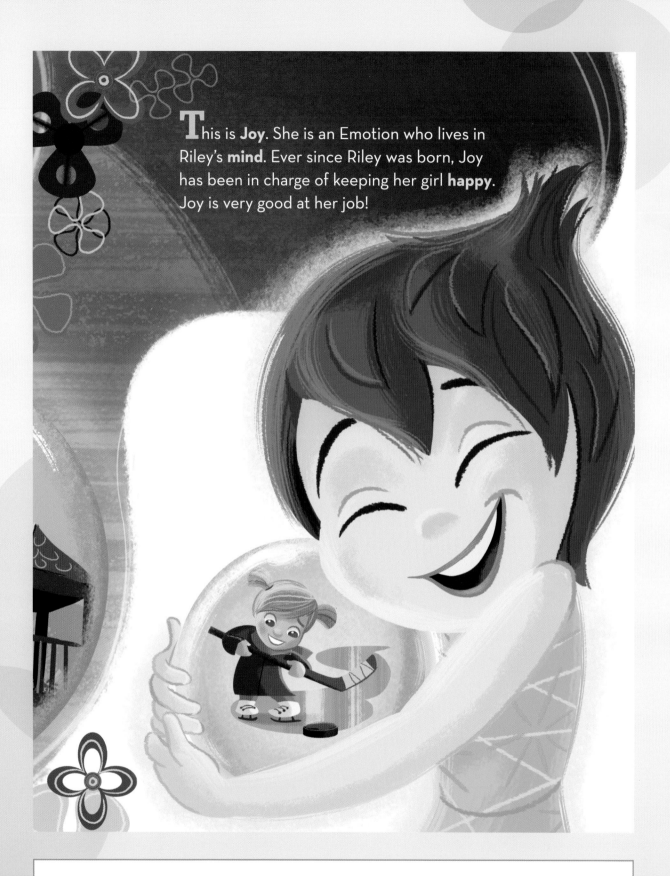

This is **Joy**. She is an Emotion who lives in Riley's **mind**. Ever since Riley was born, Joy has been in charge of keeping her girl **happy**. Joy is very good at her job!

joy : the emotion of great happiness

mind : that which is responsible for one's thoughts and feelings

happy : enjoying or showing or marked by joy or pleasure

Word	Definition

Joy works in Headquarters inside Riley's mind, along with Riley's other Emotions.

Fear helps keep Riley **safe**.

Anger helps Riley express herself if she thinks something is **unfair**—like having to eat broccoli.

Disgust helps Riley stay away from **yucky** things— like broccoli.

And then there is **Sadness**. Joy doesn't understand Sadness. She tries to keep Sadness away from the console—and from Riley's memories.

Joy works in Headquarters inside Riley's mind, along with Riley's other **Emotions**.

Fear helps keep Riley **safe**.

Anger helps Riley express herself if she thinks something is **unfair**—like having to eat broccoli.

emotion : any strong feeling

fear : an emotion experienced in anticipation of some specific pain or danger

anger : the state of being angry

Word	Definition

Disgust helps Riley **stay away** from **yucky** things—like broccoli.

And then there is **Sadness**. Joy doesn't **understand** Sadness. She tries to keep Sadness away from the console—and from Riley's memories.

stay away : stay clear of, avoid

sadness : emotions experienced when not in a state of well-being

understand : know and comprehend the nature or meaning of

Word	Definition

Joy is proud that most of Riley's memories are happy ones, and she wants to keep them that way!

The most important memories are called **core memories**. They power the **Islands of Personality**—Family Island, Honesty Island, Hockey Island, Friendship Island, and Goofball Island—and make Riley, Riley.

Everything is great until Riley and her family move to a new city.
Riley misses her friends, their new house is a mess, and the pizza
has **broccoli** on it! Riley's Emotions don't know what to do.

Joy is proud that most of Riley's **memories** are happy ones, and she wants to keep them that way!

The most important memories are called **core memories**. They **power** the **Islands of Personality**—Family Island, Honesty Island, Hockey Island, Friendship Island, and Goofball Island—and make Riley, Riley.

memory : something that is remembered

core : the central part of something

power : possession of controlling influence

Word	Definition

Everything is great until Riley and her **family** move to a new city. Riley **misses** her friends, their new house is a **mess**, and the pizza has **broccoli** on it! Riley's Emotions don't know what to do.

family : a social unit living together

miss : feel or suffer from the lack of

mess : a state of confusion and disorderliness

Word	Definition

Sadness touches a yellow memory and it turns blue! When Joy tries to stop her, all of Riley's core memories get knocked loose. Joy, Sadness, and all of the core memories get sucked out of Headquarters . . .

. . . and end up lost deep
inside Riley's mind.

Sadness touches a yellow memory and it turns blue! When Joy tries to **stop** her, all of Riley's core memories get knocked loose. Joy, Sadness, and all of the core memories get sucked out of **Headquarters** . . .

. . . and end up **lost** deep inside Riley's mind.

stop : the event of something ending

headquarters : the office that serves as the administrative center of an enterprise

lost : no longer in your possession or control

Word	Definition

Joy is worried. What will happen to Riley if she's not there to make her happy? Joy tries to stay positive. She tells Sadness they need to get back to Headquarters to return the core memories. That's the only way the Islands of Personality will work again.

Joy is **worried**. What will happen to Riley if she's not there to make her happy? Joy tries to stay **positive**. She tells Sadness they need to get back to Headquarters to return the core memories. That's the only way the Islands of **Personality** will work again.

worry : something or someone that causes anxiety

positive : characterized by or displaying affirmation or acceptance or certainty etc.

personality : the complex of all the attributes-behavioral, temperamental, emotional and mental-that characterize a unique individual

Word	Definition

Things aren't going well back at Headquarters. Without Joy to run things, the other Emotions have to take charge.

Fear, Anger, and Disgust make Riley act different. She's a sore loser at hockey tryouts.

She talks back to her parents.

At school, she sits alone and **sulks**.

Things aren't going well **back** at Headquarters. Without Joy to run things, the **other** Emotions have to take **charge**.

back : related to or located at the back

other : not the same one or ones already mentioned or implied

charge : an impetuous rush toward someone or something

Word	Definition

Fear, Anger, and **Disgust** make Riley act different. She's a sore loser at hockey **tryouts**.

She talks back to her parents.

At school, she sits alone and **sulks**.

disgust : strong feelings of dislike

tryout : put to the test, as for its quality, or give experimental use to

sulk : a mood or display of sullen aloofness or withdrawal

Word	Definition

Without her core memories in place, Riley's Islands of Personality begin to **crumble** away!

Without her core memories in place, Riley's **Islands** of Personality begin to **crumble** away!

island : a land mass that is surrounded by water

crumble : fall apart

Word	Definition

While traveling back to Headquarters, Joy and Sadness run into Riley's old imaginary friend, **Bing Bong**. He is sad because Riley has forgotten him.

Joy is surprised to see that Sadness is able to comfort Bing Bong. Perhaps Sadness is good for something after all.

Meanwhile, Anger gives Riley a terrible idea.
She is going to run away!

While traveling back to Headquarters, Joy and Sadness run into Riley's old **imaginary** friend, **Bing Bong**. He is sad because Riley has forgotten him.

Joy is surprised to see that Sadness is able to **comfort** Bing Bong. Perhaps Sadness is good for something after all.

Meanwhile, Anger gives Riley a **terrible** idea. She is going to run away!

imaginary : not based on fact

comfort : a state of being relaxed and feeling no pain

terrible : causing fear or dread or terror

Word	Definition

On their journey, Joy is surprised to find out that
she and Sadness share the same favorite memory.
It was after a hockey game back in Minnesota.
Sadness remembers that Riley missed the
winning shot and felt awful.

Joy replays the memory and sees that Riley
was really sad. But then her family and friends
made her feel better. Joy now understands
that sometimes Riley needs to be sad before
she can be happy again.

On their journey, Joy is **surprised** to find out that she and Sadness share the same **favorite** memory. It was after a hockey game back in Minnesota. Sadness remembers that Riley missed the winning shot and felt **awful**.

surprise : the astonishment you feel when something totally unexpected happens to you

favorite : appealing to the general public

awful : exceptionally bad or displeasing

Word	Definition

Joy **replays** the memory and sees that Riley was really sad. But then her family and friends made her **feel** better. Joy now understands that sometimes Riley needs to be sad before she can be happy **again**.

replay : play again

feel : an intuitive awareness

again : for another time, one more time

Word	Definition

Joy and Sadness finally make it back to Headquarters.
And they're just in time—Riley is on a bus!
Joy urges Sadness to take over the console.

Joy and Sadness finally make it back to Headquarters.
And they're just in time—Riley is on a bus!
Joy **urges** Sadness to take over the **console**.

urge : an instinctive motive

console : a flat surface that contains the controls for a machine, for a piece of electrical equipment, etc.

Word	Definition

All the Emotions watch as Sadness touches the console. Riley begins to feel sad right away. She misses her parents. She yells for the bus driver to stop.

Riley races home. She cries and tells her parents she misses Minnesota. Her parents say they miss Minnesota, too. Riley begins to feel better. She smiles through her tears.

All the Emotions watch as Sadness **touches** the console. Riley
begins to feel sad right away. She misses her parents. She **yells**
for the bus driver to stop.

touch : the event of something coming in contact with the body

yell : a loud utterance

Word	Definition

Riley races home. She **cries** and tells her parents she misses Minnesota. Her parents say they miss Minnesota, too. Riley begins to feel better. She **smiles** through her **tears**.

cry : a loud utterance of emotion

smile : a facial expression characterized by turning up the corners of the mouth

tear : a drop of the clear salty saline solution secreted by the lacrimal glands

Word	Definition

Before long, Riley adjusts to her new life in San Francisco. She has new friends, a new hockey team, and all five Emotions working together as a team.

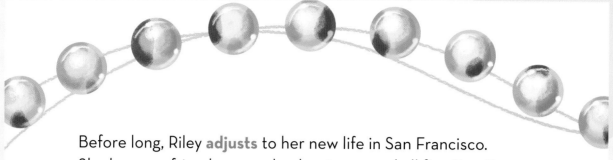

Before long, Riley **adjusts** to her new life in San Francisco. She has new friends, a new hockey **team**, and all five Emotions working **together** as a team.

adjust : alter or regulate so as to achieve accuracy or conform to a standard

team : a cooperative unit

together : with each other

Word	Definition

글 안드레아 포스너 산체스 | 그림 앨런 뱃슨

1판 1쇄 펴낸 날 | 2024년 12월 25일

펴낸이   장영재
펴낸곳   (주)미르북컴퍼니
자회사   더모던
전 화   02)3141-4421
팩 스   0505-333-4428
등 록   2012년 3월 16일(제313-2012-81호)
주 소   서울시 마포구 성미산로32길 12, 2층 (우 03983)
e-mail   sanhonjinju@naver.com
카 페   cafe.naver.com/mirbookcompany
인스타그램   www.instagram.com/mirbooks

KC인증정보 **품명** 아동 도서 **사용연령** 4~7세 **제조년월일** 2024년 12월 25일 **제조국** 대한민국 **연락처**
02)3141-4421 서울시 마포구 성미산로32길 12, 2층 **주의사항** 종이에 베이거나 긁히지 않도록 조심하세요.
책 모서리가 날카로우니 던지거나 떨어뜨리지 마세요.